Making Friends
With Breezy

The Muddy Paws series

Making Friends With Breezy

JENNY OLDFIELD

Illustrated by Paul Howard

Hodder
Children's
Books

A division of Hachette Children's Books

To Lola, Jude
and Evan –
my little stars!
JO

Chapter One

"Whoops, Dad – watch where you're going!" Lily cried.

She and her cousin, Lexi, had to jump to one side as Matt cycled towards them along the narrow country lane.

He braked hard and stopped. "Sorry about that, girls. Have you had a good day at school?"

"Brilliant, thanks," Lexi said. Then she frowned and pointed to the black helmet hanging from the handlebars of his bright green mountain bike. "Uncle Matt, why aren't you wearing it?"

"Yes, Dad, why aren't you?" Lily echoed.

"I was in a hurry to get to the post office. I need to send this parcel before it closes." He raised his arm to pat the package sticking out of his rucksack.

"Wear your helmet!" Lexi and Lily cried, hands on hips. They stepped out and blocked his way until he'd done as they said.

"You're right," he sighed as he put his helmet on. "Anyway, Lexi, your dad called to say he'll be home tomorrow evening. And by the way, Jo answered a phone call about a sick cat."

"Cool!" Lexi grinned. She was looking forward to being with her dad at their house just outside Mellingham. And it seemed there would soon be a new client for her and Lily to deal with at Muddy Paws.

"What's wrong with the cat?" Lily wanted to know.

"Don't know – you'll have to ask Mum."
Matt really was in a hurry as he fastened the
helmet and got ready to pedal.

"We will," Lily promised, eager to get
home. "Come on, Lexi!"

The two girls grinned, stood aside and
waved Matt on his way.

"Yippee – only one more schoolday to
go!" Lily called after him.

"And then it's the summer holidays!" Lexi
cried. "Come on, Lily – I'll race you!"

* * *

"Let me guess – it's a cat with a fur ball stuck
in its throat." Lily sat in Sea View Café,
quizzing her mum.

Jo came to the table with two slices of
cherry cake for the girls. There were three
other people in the café – Mark Simons and
his twin sons, Sam and Jon. "I don't know

exactly what's wrong," she told Lily. "But the cat's name is Dino, so 'it' is definitely a 'he'."

"Hmm, Dino." Lexi decided that she liked the name. "Who does he belong to?"

"I got the call from Daisy Goodwin. She's the lady who's just moved in to number six Lighthouse Cottages."

"I hope you told her to bring Dino to Muddy Paws," Lily mumbled, her mouth full of cake. For two months she and Lexi had run the agency in their spare time. Soon, when the summer holidays began, they would have lots of free days to help people with their problem pets.

Jo nodded as she brought drinks for Mark and his eight-year-old boys. "I told her tomorrow at four thirty."

"Great!" Lily and Lexi smiled and munched.

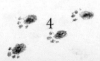

4

Jon Simons was listening in. "Muddy Paws?" he asked.

"We help people with their pets," Lexi told him proudly. "We can train dogs to behave nicely on the lead."

"Or teach them not to fight with other dogs," Lily added.

"We'll help you find your missing cat," Lexi went on.

"Wow!" Jon was impressed. He turned to his brother. "Are you thinking what I'm thinking?"

Sam nodded. "What about a guinea pig?" he asked Lily and Lexi.

"Sure – we help guinea pigs," Lily told him. "Why?"

"It's Hubert," Jon explained

"He's very fat," Sam said with a serious expression.

"We need to put him on a diet."

"OK, let's take a look," Lexi decided. "Definitely bring him to Muddy Paws."

"How about this time tomorrow?" Lily asked with a wide grin.

* * *

The last day of term whizzed by for Lily and Lexi.

"Take your pictures off the walls, roll them nicely and put them in your bags." Mrs Taylor gave out instructions. "Lily and Lexi, remember to take Smudge home with you for the first two weeks of the holidays."

"How could we forget?" Lily was thrilled that the teacher had chosen Muddy Paws to look after the creamy-coloured hamster. Carefully she picked up Smudge's cage and stood by the door. "He's so cu-u-ute!"

When the bell went, she and Lexi were

first out into the playground.

"Bye, everyone!" they called to their friends. "See you in September!"

And they hurried out of the school gates to find Lexi's dad and her dog, Alfie, waiting for them.

"Surprise!" James, Lexi's dad, cried. Alfie wagged his tail.

She shrieked and flung her arms around

her dad's neck. "You're not supposed to be here yet!"

"I caught an earlier plane," he grinned, only putting her down when she was dizzy.

"Hi, Alfie!" Scooping him up, Lexi kissed her dog on the top of his silky black head. "Dad, can you drop us off at Lily's house? We've got to look after Smudge, and we have to help Jon and Sam get Hubert on a diet then after that we have to see Dino . . ."

"Whoa!" James laughed as he helped Lily and Lexi into his car. Alfie scrambled in after them and sat at Lexi's feet.

Lily placed Smudge's cage on the seat and strapped him in. "Hi, Uncle James."

"Hi, Lily. As you can see, my daughter's much too busy with her precious animals to find time for her poor old dad!"

"We are – we're big-time busy!" Lily told

him how Muddy Paws had really taken off. "It started when we coached Madcap for Mellingham Show."

Madcap the Jack Russell pup had been their biggest success so far. In two weeks they'd turned him from a yipping, yapping little rascal into a prize-winning show dog for his famous, pop star owner.

"And quite right too," Lexi's dad said. "I'm happy for you."

"So come and have tea in the café," Lily suggested.

"While Lily and I sort out some more problem pets," Lexi added.

Guinea pigs and cats, kittens and hamsters, ponies and puppies – no problem was too big or too small for Lily and Lexi at Muddy Paws!

Chapter Two

"Hubert needs to eat grass, hay and lettuce," Lily told the Simons twins.

The chubby black guinea pig sat glumly on Jon's lap in the old stable in the Sea View paddock.

"He *is* very fat," Lexi said. "What else do you give him?"

"Cornflakes," Sam admitted.

"And cake," Jon added.

"No more cake!" Lily knew they had to be strict. "But you can give him kiwi fruit. That's good for him."

"OK." It was time for the twins to leave. Jon put poor Hubert in his cage. "Your T-shirts are cool," he told Lily. "I like the logo."

She smiled and tugged at the hem of her T-shirt to straighten it so that the twins got a better view of the paw print design and rainbow letters which spelt out the name, Muddy Paws.

"Bring Hubert back next week," Lexi suggested. "We'll take another look at him then."

* * *

"So what's wrong with Dino?" Lexi asked Daisy Goodwin.

The pure white Persian cat was curled up inside his pet carrier, gazing out with enormous, sad green eyes.

Miss Goodwin patted her neat grey hair

into place then sighed. "He's not himself. He lies in his basket all day long. Then when I have visitors, he slinks off and hides behind the curtains."

"Is he eating OK?" Lily wanted to know.

"Not really. He seems to have lost his appetite."

"Did you take him to the vet?" Lexi was anxious because Dino looked so sorry for himself.

"Yes. She told me she couldn't find anything wrong."

"Hmm." Lily thought hard. "We need to read up about this," she told Dino's worried owner.

"We'll find out what to do to make him feel better," Lexi assured her.

"I've tried everything I can think of," Miss Goodwin sighed, lifting Dino's carrier from the table. The sad, fluffy cat gave a little miaow.

"We'll do our best," Lily promised.

"We *definitely* will." Lexi planned to surf the net until they came up with an answer. "We'll call you as soon as we can."

* * *

"OK, Alfie – walkies!" After Miss Goodwin and Dino had gone, Lexi stood with Lily on the lawn at the back of the café and called her little dog.

Alfie bounded towards her, a happy bundle of white and black fur.

"Come on, Alfie. We just have time for a walk before the sun goes down." Lily led the way along the footpath towards the beach. Passing Lighthouse Cottages, they came to the side gate leading into the grounds of Dentwood Hall where they stopped to say hello to the three peacocks living there. The male bird puffed out his electric-blue chest and spread his beautiful tail feathers. He let out a high-pitched screech – "E-e-elp! E-e-elp!"

"Woof!" Alfie urged from further along the path.

"Hang on, Alfie – we're coming!" Lexi laughed.

Soon they came to the wooden steps leading down to the beach. Alfie scampered ahead.

"Wait for us," Lily begged. No way could the girls keep up.

He was still ahead of them, already splashing at the water's edge when Lexi and Lily rolled up their jeans and stepped on to the warm sand. The waves broke and curled on to the shore, and the sea sparkled in the evening light.

"Alfie's found a friend." Lexi was the first to spot the golden retriever that lolloped up to little Alfie, tail wagging. "It looks like Molly from the Hall."

They raced to the shore then waded in to the foaming water to join the dogs.

"Brrr!" Lexi shivered.

"Watch out – here comes Monty!" Lily recognized the big chestnut horse that galloped towards them from the far end of the beach. His hooves thundered along the shoreline, kicking up wet sand.

"Hi, Mrs Finch!" Lexi waved as horse and rider drew near.

"Hello, girls." The owner of Dentwood Hall reined Monty back. She stopped for a quick chat. "It's a lovely evening."

Lily shaded her eyes with her hands. "Monty's so strong and fast," she sighed.

The chestnut horse breathed heavily after his gallop. His neck was arched and he pranced on the spot.

"He's lovely, isn't he?" Mrs Finch smiled down at the girls and the dogs. "You must visit him at the Hall. Perhaps you'd like to meet Phoebe, our Shetland pony, too."

"Wow!" Lexi gasped.

"Yes, please!" Lily jumped at the chance.

"Has either of you been around horses before?" Rosemary Finch asked as she tugged the peak of her hard hat further down her forehead.

Lexi and Lily shook their heads. Cats,

dogs, hamsters, guinea pigs – yes. Horses – no.

"But you're not frightened of them?"

They shook their heads while Alfie and Molly romped through the shallow waves.

"Visit us tomorrow," Rosemary decided. "You can meet Phoebe, and while you're there I promise to show you someone else very special."

"Thanks, Mrs Finch!" For once Lexi and Lily were lost for words.

"Good, that's settled." Calling Molly to heel, Rosemary Finch got ready to ride on. "Tomorrow morning at nine," she called over her shoulder as Monty galloped on.

Chapter Three

"Domestic cat – health problems." Lily typed the words then pressed "Search".

Lexi peered over her shoulder and read what came up on the computer screen. "Fur balls, grooming problems – no, neither of those fit Dino," she said. "Isn't there something about cats who lie around all day and hide behind curtains?"

"Wait," Lily told her.

Lexi and Alfie had showed up early at Sea View, ready for their visit to Dentwood Hall. It was Lily who'd reminded her about

Miss Goodwin's cat. "We promised we'd call her, remember."

"Fleas – no." Lexi read on. "Skin rashes – no."

"Oh, but look." Lily pointed the cursor at a box which read "Loss of appetite" then she ran down a list of possible causes. "Miss Goodwin told us that Dino didn't eat much. It says here that it can be caused by stress."

"Stress?" Lexi frowned. "Such as?"

"Such as other cats coming into the house," Lily read.

"No. Miss Goodwin didn't mention that."

"Or the owner *moving* house." Lily rested the cursor on the last item on the list. "Didn't Mum say that Miss Goodwin had just moved into Lighthouse Cottages?"

"Yeah!" Lexi cried. "Lily, you're a genius for remembering that!"

"'A cat who moves house can suffer from stress,'" Lily read aloud. "'They become listless and anxious. Such cats are clinically depressed.'"

"That's it!" Straight away Lexi picked up the phone but when she rang Miss Goodwin's number there was no reply.

"Leave a message," Lily told her, looking at her watch. "Say we'll call in later this morning. Come on, Lexi – it's almost nine o'clock."

* * *

"Elp! Elp! Elp!" the peacocks cried from the lawn at the back of Dentwood Hall.

Rosemary Finch opened the gate to welcome Lexi and Lily. "Peacocks are better than any guard dog," she told them with a bright smile.

"Woof!" Big Molly bounded out to meet

Alfie. Her bark was deep and loud.

Alfie cocked his head and looked up at Lexi.

"It's OK, you two can go and play," she told him.

So Molly and Alfie raced off around the side of the grand house, ahead of Mrs Finch, Lily and Lexi. "Let me show you the stables," the owner of the Hall said. "Most of them are empty now, since my son, Harry, decided he's not interested in horses, I'm afraid."

"Elp!" The peacocks' piercing cry could still be heard as they entered the stable yard.

Lexi nudged Lily as she caught sight of a dark-haired boy getting ready to throw a ball for Molly and Alfie. But as soon as he noticed the visitors, he dropped the ball and disappeared.

"Monty is in the first stable." Mrs Finch

seemed happy to lead the girls on a guided tour. "He's a retired racehorse – a thoroughbred, of course."

"You're gorgeous!" Lexi snuck in a compliment as she walked by.

Monty snickered and clunked the door with his hoof a second time.

"And here's Phoebe's stable." Stopping halfway down the row, Mrs Finch opened a white door and stepped inside. Ten seconds later she led out a tiny brown and white pony with a shaggy mane and a big, round belly. "Phoebe's a grand old lady now."

"Oh, cute!" Lexi went up to pat the pony. "Look at her tiny hooves."

"You can hardly see her eyes behind that thick mane," Lily grinned.

Cheeky Phoebe nosed in Lexi's pocket.

"She's looking for a treat," Mrs Finch

explained. Then, with a twinkle in her eye she made a suggestion. "There's a bag of carrots in the stable at the end of the row. Why don't you go and find one?"

Lexi and Lily ran to fetch Phoebe's treat.

"Take your time," Mrs Finch called as Lily got ready to slide back the bolt. "There's no hurry."

Lexi hesitated and peered over the door.

She heard a soft rustling sound from inside the stable. "Did you hear that?"

Lily nodded. "Someone's in there."

"Or some*thing*." Gradually Lexi's eyes got used to the dim light. She made out a bed of clean straw and a shallow dish.

The rustling soon stopped and then there was silence. "Is it another Shetland pony?" Lily wondered.

Lexi called softly. "Who's there?" Maybe it was Harry Finch, hiding from them, ready to spring out.

"Open the door, go in and see," Mrs Finch suggested.

So Lexi slid back the bolt and the girls stepped inside.

"Oh!" Lily gasped and stood fixed to the spot.

"O-o-o-h!" Lexi echoed.

There, on the bed of straw lay the tiniest, fluffiest, most beautiful chestnut foal they'd ever seen.

"Meet the newest member of our family at Dentwood Hall," Mrs Finch said as she stepped into the stable and closed the door behind her. "Her name is Summer Breeze – Breezy for short."

Chapter Four

Summer Breeze lay with her skinny legs folded under her. Her big brown eyes looked startled.

"Don't go too close," Mrs Finch warned as she joined the girls. "Breezy's shy around strangers."

"Hello, Breezy!" Lexi murmured.

Lily could hardly believe how beautiful the foal was. "Everything is so mini!"

Breezy had tiny hooves and a stumpy little tail, a fluffy mane, pricked-up ears and a white star on her forehead.

"Don't you just love her!" Lexi exclaimed. For both girls, it was love at first sight.

"How old is she?" Lily wanted to know.

"She was born six weeks ago," Rosemary told them. "Monty is her father, but of course stallions don't want anything to do with their offspring after they're born."

"And where's her mum?" Lily whispered as Summer Breeze stood up from her straw bed and eyed them nervously.

"Ah, that's a sad story, I'm afraid." Gently moving the dish of milk closer to the foal, Rosemary waited until she began to drink. "Her mother was a beautiful grey mare called Summer Haze but unfortunately she died soon after Breezy was born."

"That's terrible," Lexi murmured. "Poor little Breezy!"

"She had to be bottle-fed right from the

start. It's been a hard slog and I know for a fact that she misses her mother."

"Do you give her anything besides milk?" Lily asked, watching every movement Breezy made. The foal seemed to drink thirstily, only glancing up every now and then to make sure that her visitors didn't crowd in on her.

"I've got her on to solid food – pellets soaked in goat's milk. She eats a huge amount. She has to because she's growing so fast."

"She's amazing," Lexi sighed.

"Would you like to help me to prepare Breezy's next meal?" Rosemary asked.

Lexi and Lily nodded then followed her out into the yard where Alfie and Molly were playing and the three peacocks pecked at grain.

"We store Breezy's feed in the tack room."

Rosemary walked briskly across the cobbled yard into an outbuilding where she poured pellets into a bowl then added milk. "We give it a stir," she said, "and hey presto – breakfast!"

Then it was back with the feed to the foal's stable. "Open the door gently," Rosemary told Lexi as she handed the bowl to Lily. "Then go in and put it down where she can see it."

So Lily tiptoed into the stable, taking care not to scare Breezy. She placed the feed on the stone floor then slowly backed out.

"Well done," Rosemary told her. As they stood and watched the foal sniff at the bowl and begin to feed, her owner sighed. "If only everyone could be as calm with her as you've been, life would be so much easier."

* * *

"Please can we . . . I mean, may we . . . come

again?" Lily stammered as Lexi went to fetch Alfie and she followed Rosemary Finch out of the foal's stable.

"Any time you like," Rosemary replied cheerfully.

"Tomorrow?"

"Definitely. Or later today. I mean it – whenever you want."

"Thanks, Mrs Finch. Thanks, thanks, thanks! We won't be a nuisance, honest. We just can't wait to see Breezy again."

The owner of Dentwood Hall stopped to pat Phoebe then looked in on Monty as they passed by. "Everyone falls in love with Breezy," she told Lily. "The problem is, Breezy is unusually timid. She needs to trust you before she'll let you come anywhere near her."

Lily nodded. That *was* a big problem, she agreed.

"You have to be gentle and take your time," Rosemary insisted.

"Do you think she would let me stroke her?" Lily dared to ask.

"You can try," Mrs Finch agreed. She opened the foal's door and let Lily into the stable. "Go in – that's right, nice and gently. Go up to her slowly but don't look

her in the eye – horses don't like that if they don't know you very well."

Lily eased forward and was about to reach out to touch Breezy's soft, tufty mane when a sudden noise from the yard made the trembling foal jump back into the furthest corner.

"Mum!" a boy's voice called from behind

the tack room and Harry Finch sped into view on his mountain bike. With a squeal of brakes he jumped off the bike and let it clatter on to the cobbles. "Why did you let Molly loose with that other dog? Did you know they jumped in the pond and scared the ducks . . .?"

Seeing Lily by Monty's stable, Harry suddenly stopped and scowled.

"Calm down, Harry. I'm sure everything's fine," his mum said.

Then a blushing Lexi appeared with a dripping Alfie at her side. "Sorry about that," she told Mrs Finch. "Alfie isn't usually naughty."

His ears drooped and he hung his head as he shook himself dry.

Rosemary smiled. "We'll see you later, perhaps," she told Lily.

"Definitely!" Lily promised. "And next time, Lexi can try to stroke Breezy as well." She said bye to Harry as she ran to join Lexi but he shrugged and turned away.

"What's eating him?" Lexi asked as they made their way down the drive and out between the tall iron gates.

Lily shrugged. "Who cares? Anyway, it's time to sort Dino out."

"You bet," Lexi told her. "Come on, Alfie – this is another case for Muddy Paws!"

* * *

Rat-tat-a-tat-tat! Lexi knocked on Daisy Goodwin's door. "Alfie, sit!" she said. "Stay!"

He wagged his damp tail and sat.

Miss Goodwin opened her door. "Come in. I'm so glad you're here. Poor Dino is getting worse."

Lily led the way and Lexi followed while

Alfie sat patiently on the path.

"Look at him," Miss Goodwin sighed.

It was true – Dino looked even sadder than before, curled up in his basket without moving.

"So what do you think is the matter with him?"

Lily frowned and hesitated. How did you explain to an owner that their cat had a bad case of stress?

"Dino's depressed." Lexi came straight out with it. "It's because you moved house."

"Depressed?" Miss Goodwin murmured, bending to pick Dino up.

"He's not eating, he doesn't want to play. All he wants to do is sleep." Lily gave her a list of symptoms. "We looked up the things that can go wrong with cats and this is the one that fits him best."

"Depressed," Miss Goodwin said, this time with a sigh. "How do we cure that?"

"Ah!" Lexi thought she had the answer. She'd read more on the website last night after she and her dad had left Sea View and gone home. "You could try aro . . . arom . . . aromatherapy."

Lily stared at her. "What does that even mean?" she muttered.

"It's where you use oils that smell nice. If Dino's got stress you have to dab a few drops of lavender oil on his bed. It's very calming."

Doubtfully Lily raised her eyebrows but Miss Goodwin looked relieved as she put Dino back in his basket then went to a kitchen drawer and began to search. "I know exactly what you mean. Aromatherapy works well on humans so I see no reason

why it shouldn't work on cats. I think I may even have a bottle of lavender oil in here."

Lexi smiled and nodded while Lily crouched to stroke Dino's soft white fur.

"Yes, here we are!" Unscrewing the cap, Miss Goodwin took a long sniff. "In fact, I used to pour a few drops into a bucket of water whenever I sponged Honeysuckle down after a long ride along the bridleways."

"Do you like horses?" Lexi asked eagerly as Miss Goodwin dabbed the oil on to Dino's bed. And she rushed to tell her all about Monty and Phoebe at Dentwood Hall.

"And you should have seen Summer Breeze!" Lily sighed. "She's only six weeks old and she lost her mum."

"It's sad but she's so-o-o cute!" Lexi sighed. "We're going back to see her, and try and stroke her."

"Even though Mrs Finch says she's really shy."

"Yes," Miss Goodwin said. "It's hard to bond with orphan foals."

"She's so nervous," Lexi murmured.

"And scared of loud noises," Lily added sadly.

"She's lonely without her mum," Lexi explained.

"But we'll definitely make friends with her in the end." Lily was determined to succeed.

"Later today," Lily added. "After we've helped Mum bake cakes for the café, fed Smudge some fresh vegetables and updated our website for Muddy Paws."

Chapter Five

The smell of baking filled the kitchen at Sea View. Jo had just taken a banana cake and a Victoria sponge out of the oven.

Alfie lay beside the Aga, soaking up the warmth, while Lexi and Lily tidied away flour and sugar, eggs and butter.

Jo hummed a tune as she loaded the dishwasher. "Thank you, girls – that was a great help."

Lily loved baking with her mum because it gave them time to chat. "Lexi posted news about Dino and Hubert on our Muddy Paws

41

website," she'd told Jo as they baked.

"I want to take a picture of Breezy later today," Lexi had added. "Then I can put it on the website."

"Who's Breezy?" Jo had asked.

And they'd fallen over themselves in their hurry to tell her about Rosemary Finch's foal.

"So what's next for Muddy Paws?" Jo asked now that the baking was done and she'd wiped the surfaces clean.

"We're going to give Smudge this dish of carrots." Lily had already chopped the healthy treat into small chunks.

"Then we're taking Alfie for a walk on the beach," Lexi went on. "And on the way back we're . . ."

"No – let me guess. You're calling in on Breezy!" Jo got it right first time.

"Is that OK? Or do you need us to do stuff in the café?" Lily checked.

"Go!" Jo laughed. "Go on, shoo! And tell Rosemary Finch I said hi!"

* * *

"Hi, girls – I've been expecting you." Rosemary was busy in the stable yard when Lexi, Lily and Alfie arrived. She unbuckled Monty's girth and lifted the saddle from his back.

Harry was there too but when he saw the visitors he skulked away.

"Ignore him," his mum sighed. "He's in a worse mood than usual because I've just told him that I have to go away for a few days."

"How's Breezy?" Lily asked while Lexi went to Phoebe's stable and said hi.

"She's doing well. We had a little panic earlier this afternoon when I tried to put a head collar on for the first time. She didn't like it at all."

Lily and Lexi waited while Rosemary led Monty into his stable. When she came out she told them it was time for Breezy to be fed again.

The girls ran to the tack room to help prepare the feed.

"That's right – two good scoops of pellets," Rosemary told Lily. "Now Lexi, add a litre of goat's milk and stir."

"This is better than baking cakes!" Lexi giggled as she stirred hard.

"I'll let you take it into Breezy's stable again," Rosemary decided. She watched as Lily opened the foal's door and Lexi carried the bowl inside. "Nice and easy," she breathed.

From the corner of the stable Breezy

watched warily. She waited until Lexi and Lily had gone out and closed the door before she ventured forward to eat.

"Why is she scared of us?" Lexi asked Rosemary with a worried frown.

"She's scared of everyone except me, I'm afraid. And that's only because I was the one who looked after her when her mum died."

"But will she get used to us?" Lily was still longing for the time when she could go up to Breezy and stroke her.

"In time," Rosemary promised.

For a while they all watched the foal munch the pellets. Further along the row, Monty kicked his hoof against his door and Phoebe poked her shaggy head out of her stable and snickered. Then Molly bounded into the yard and woofed at Alfie. Soon the two dogs raced off to play.

"Girls," Rosemary began. She sounded as if she'd been thinking hard. "I was wondering if you would do me a favour."

"Sure," Lily said.

"What is it?" Lexi asked.

"I mentioned that I have to go away for a few days at the start of next week – well, how would it be if I gave you the job of coming in to feed Breezy?"

Lily gasped. "That would be brilliant!"

"My husband, George, will be here with Harry, of course. They can take care of Monty and Phoebe, that's no problem. But Breezy is different. The poor little thing seems to be frightened by George's deep voice. As for Harry – well, you've seen how he dashes everywhere and makes lots of noise."

"We have and we'll do it!" Lexi declared. She didn't even pause to think.

"Muddy Paws would love to feed Summer Breeze!" Lily told Rosemary, her chest puffed out with pride.

* * *

That night Matt and James helped Lily and Lexi put up pictures of Breezy on the Muddy Paws website.

"This is a lot to take on," Lexi's dad warned when he heard about Rosemary's plan for the girls to feed Breezy. "Have you ever dealt with a foal before?"

"No, but Mrs Finch showed us how to do it," Lexi told him.

"You go slowly into the stable," Lily explained. "You don't do anything sudden."

"Just take care you don't get kicked," Matt said.

"Breezy's tiny," Lexi reminded the two worried dads. "She's only six weeks old."

"Even so." James agreed with Matt. "Those little hooves can pack a punch."

"We'll be careful," Lexi promised.

Lily pointed to the close-up picture of Breezy's beautiful face. "Look at her – I just want to stroke her and cuddle her and hug her to bits!" she sighed.

* * *

Sunday whizzed by. Muddy Paws was busy with Jigsaw, the King Charles spaniel who wanted to chase sheep, and Smudge, whose cage had to be cleaned. Lexi lifted the hamster's wheel on to Lily's kitchen table and let him play while Lily put in new bedding.

"Whoops!" she cried when Smudge jumped down from the table on to the floor. He was scuttling towards the open door when Lexi scooped him up. "Oh no you don't!"

At three o'clock they had unexpected visitors when Sam and Jon Simons came knocking.

"We've brought Hubert back," Sam explained.

"It's urgent," Jon added.

The fair-haired twins blushed as they brought Hubert's cage into the kitchen.

"Dad's waiting for us in the car," Sam went on.

"Why, what happened?" Lily wanted to know. "Didn't Hubert like his new healthy diet?"

"It's not that." Jon opened Hubert's cage and lifted him out. "We're giving him hay and grass and kiwi fruit just like you said."

"He likes it," Sam said. "It's just that our Aunty Julie came to our house today and she knows a lot about guinea pigs.

She picked Hubert up and kind of turned him upside down."

"He squeaked," Jon told them.

"I'm not surprised," Lexi said. "You'd squeak too if we turned you upside down."

"Only he's not a he," Sam explained.

"He's a *she*," Jon added.

"A *she*!" Lily said.

"We've changed her name to Harriet." Sam blushed furiously.

"Harriet isn't just fat from eating too much," Jon said. "Aunty Julie says she's having babies."

"Babies?" Lexi cried.

They stared wide-eyed at the white guinea pig sitting on the kitchen table.

"Your guinea pig's pregnant! Why didn't we think of that?" Lily groaned.

"Because we thought Hubert was a *he*," Lexi pointed out. She felt her own face flush bright red. "But Harriet is a *she*! Whoever would've guessed!"

Chapter Six

"Daisy Goodwin says thanks for Dino's lavender oil. It definitely seems to be working," Matt told Lily next morning.

"That's cool, Dad." Lily was in a hurry. It was time to meet Lexi and Alfie and head off to Dentwood Hall. "See you later!"

She found Lexi waiting at the end of her drive and soon they were running along the footpath leading to the Hall.

"Two scoops of pellets and a litre of goat's milk." Lexi rehearsed the recipe for Breezy's breakfast as they ducked under low branches

and brushed against the prickly hedgerow.

"E-e-lp!" the peacocks cried when Lily opened the Hall gate. The male puffed out his brilliant blue chest while the dowdy peahens pecked at the grass.

"Oh, it's you," Harry Finch grunted as Lily and Lexi rushed into the stable yard. He was wearing a baseball cap, a yellow T-shirt and green wellies, wheeling a barrow full of muck away from Monty's stable.

Hi, Harry! Lexi thought. *We're happy to see you too!*

A tall, dark-haired man strode out of the tack room. "You must be Lexi and Lily," he said in his deep, gruff voice. "You're from Muddy Paws and you've come to feed Breezy?"

"That's us." Lily pointed to the logo on her T-shirt.

"Well, the farrier is due here shortly so I'll leave you to it," George Finch told them as he disappeared into Monty's stable.

Once inside the tack room, Lexi measured out Breezy's pellets. "Two scoops."

"One litre." Lily poured the milk into the bowl.

"Give it a good stir," Lexi reminded her.

"Ready!" Lily announced. "Are you nervous?"

"A bit," Lexi admitted as they reached

Breezy's door. "We have to make sure we don't scare her."

Slowly she eased back the bolt and opened the door. Summer Breeze lay on her bed. She raised her head as the girls went in then stood up with wisps of straw in her fluffy mane and tail.

"She's a bit wobbly," Lexi whispered. "It's OK, Breezy – here's your breakfast."

The foal backed into the corner of her stable.

"I'm going to put the bowl just here," Lily murmured. "It's yummy. Come and have a taste."

"We're just going to stand here and watch you eat," Lexi added.

They had to wait ages while a white van arrived in the yard and there were sounds of the farrier unloading his tools. Each clink of metal sent Breezy cowering back into her dark corner.

"I know – you don't like the noise." Lily hoped that her voice would calm the foal. "But don't be scared – it's only the man who has come to put new shoes on Monty."

"Look, she's getting braver." Lexi kept her fingers crossed as at last Breezy ventured towards the dish and began to eat.

"Yummy!" Lily said again.

Breezy ate until the dish was empty then she looked up at the girls.

"All gone," Lexi said. "Good girl!"

The foal cocked her head to one side and took a small step towards them.

"I don't have any more," Lily told her.

But little Breezy was growing bolder. She took two more steps.

"See!" Lexi spread her empty hands,

palms upwards.

Another step and by now Breezy was so close that Lily could have reached out and touched her. "You're so sweet!" she sighed.

Breezy stretched her neck and put her soft muzzle against Lily's hand.

"She's telling us she wants more!" Lexi whispered.

"Later," Lily told her. She kept perfectly still to see what Breezy would do next.

The foal nuzzled then licked Lily's hand. Then she turned towards Lexi.

"All gone," Lexi said again, longing to stroke Breezy's soft neck. But she knew she had to let her make the first move.

It was just at that moment that Harry wheeled his empty barrow back into the yard, letting it clatter on to the cobbles as he dashed to talk to the farrier.

58

Breezy jumped and skittered away from the girls, back into her corner.

"Oh!" Lexi sighed. "I almost got to stroke her!"

"Next time," Lily vowed, although it seemed to her that she'd been hoping this for ages and ages.

Lexi called for Alfie, who came running into the yard with Molly. They said goodbye to Monty, standing calmly as the farrier took off his old shoes and pared his hooves with a giant file. Goodbye to Molly, who woofed and wagged her tail. Goodbye even to Harry Finch, who just scowled and acted like he hadn't heard.

"E-e-elp!" cried the peacocks as they crossed the back lawn.

"See you later!" Lexi and Lily closed the gate behind them and turned for home.

Chapter Seven

Lily took a sheet of paper and made a list of things to do:

Feed Smudge

Take Alfie for walk

Check up on Hubert (oops, Harriet!)

Check up on Dino

Feed Breezy

She liked lists, especially when she and Lexi had done a job and they could put a tick beside it. Feed Smudge – tick. Take Alfie for a walk – tick. Check up on Harriet.

"Hi, Sam – this is Lexi from Muddy

Paws." It was just before lunch when Lexi found time to call the Simons twins.

"It's not Sam – it's Jon."

"Oh – hi, Jon. Lily and I were wondering how Hub— sorry, Harriet is."

"She's fine," he replied. "We took her to the vet and she had a scan."

"The kind where they can see if she's pregnant?"

"Yeah – ultrasound. Anyway, she definitely is. The vet says she's going to have three babies."

"That's so cool," Lexi told him, giving Lily a thumbs-up. Three baby guinea pigs sounded like good news to her.

Jon didn't answer straight away.

"You are pleased, aren't you?"

"I don't know. What are we supposed to do with the babies if Mum and Dad won't let us keep them?"

"Hmm." Lexi thought for a while. "Hey, why don't you let us advertise them on the Muddy Paws website?"

Lily nodded and returned Lexi's thumbs-up. *Great idea!*

"Cool," Jon quickly agreed. "I'll tell Sam."

"And let us know when Harriet has her babies," Lexi insisted. "We'd love to see them as soon as they're born!"

* * *

"Check up on Dino." Lily read the next item on the list straight after lunch.

"Muddy Paws is keeping you very busy," Matt commented as the girls got ready to drop in on Miss Goodwin. "Are you sure you don't need a break?"

"No way!" they cried. They didn't have to say anything else because they both agreed

– setting up Muddy Paws was the best thing they'd ever done.

They called Alfie and left Sea View, running to Lighthouse Cottages where they knocked on Miss Goodwin's door. The old lady opened it with a smile.

"How's Dino?" Lexi asked.

"Much better, thanks to you. Come in and see."

So they went into the cosy, sweet-smelling kitchen overlooking the bright blue sea and found Dino sitting in the sun on the windowsill.

"The lavender oil must be working because he's starting to take an interest in his new surroundings," Miss Goodwin pointed out.

"Has he been outside yet?" Lily wanted to know.

"No, but he's much perkier. He ate a whole tin of sardines for breakfast."

"Cool," Lexi said.

And Lily ticked Dino off her list.

* * *

"Feed Breezy." Lily and Lexi didn't need to read the list to remember the next item. In fact, they sprinted all the way to Dentwood Hall.

They found George Finch getting into his car. "Hello, girls. I have to drive into Mellingham for a business meeting. Do you think you can manage Breezy without my help?"

"Definitely," they told him, trying not to notice Harry scowling as he kicked a football against the tack room wall – *kick-bang-bounce, kick-bang*.

"Our housekeeper, Mrs Hutchens, is in

the house if you need anything," George said as he drove away.

Lexi and Lily grinned. It felt good to be left without a grown-up looking over their shoulders.

"We can take our time," Lily said.

Lexi agreed. "Maybe today Breezy will let us stroke her."

So they got to work in the tack room, carefully measuring the pellets and milk before they carried the dish to the foal's stable.

As usual nosy Phoebe poked her head over her door and snickered.

"Hey, Pheebs!" Lexi waved. "Hey, Monty!"

The chestnut thoroughbred kicked at his door as Harry ran into the yard. With a sly look on his face he chucked his football down on the ground and kept a careful watch on Lexi and Lily.

Why is he spying on us? Lily wondered.

Lexi ignored him and slid the bolt on Breezy's door. "Sit!" she told Alfie.

Alfie sat and looked up at her with bright eyes.

"E-e-elp!" the Dentwood peacocks wailed from the back lawn.

"Hi, Breezy!" Lily carried in the foal's midday feed.

For once Breezy didn't hide away in the corner. Instead she rustled through the straw towards the girls.

"Hi!" Lexi murmured. "Here we are again."

Breezy came right up to Lily and stuck her nose in the dish before Lily had a chance to put it down. She ate greedily and sucked up every last drop of milk. Then she nuzzled Lexi's hand, looking for more.

Lexi smiled. Ever so gently she turned her hand and let Breezy sniff. More gently still she touched Breezy's cheek with her fingertips. "Does this tickle?" she asked.

Breezy sighed loudly and leaned her cheek against Lexi's hand.

"She likes it," Lily breathed, leaning over the door to warn Alfie to be quiet.

"Sshh, Alfie – we're busy. Don't whine!"

Alfie raised his front paw and scratched at the door. He whined again. Then he turned and ran a few steps, came back and whined again.

"I think something's wrong – Alfie wants us to follow him," Lily told Lexi with a puzzled frown.

"OK, Breezy, we have to go," Lexi said

softly. She and Lily slid quietly out of the stable to find Alfie waiting for them by the tack room. There was no sign of Harry – only his football lying in a corner.

"E-e-e-elp!" the peacocks cried faintly.

Alfie yelped and sprinted across the empty lawn.

"Elp! Elp!" The cry was fainter still.

Lily and Lexi ran after Alfie towards the side gate leading on to the footpath. Their

hearts were in their mouths as they realized that the three peacocks were nowhere to be seen.

"Who left the gate open?" Lexi gasped.

"Not us!" Lily was sure she'd closed it after her as they came in.

Alfie sped ahead. "Good boy, Alfie!" Lexi called. "Find the peacocks!"

The girls ran so hard they were soon out of breath. They reached the footpath in time to see little Alfie rounding up the three big birds and herding them back towards the garden.

"Watch out!" Lily stepped aside as the peacocks darted through the gate.

Lexi let Alfie herd them in then slammed the gate shut. "Good boy!" she said again.

"Phew!" Lily took a deep breath. She made sure the peacocks were back where they should be, happily pecking at the grass. Then she glanced up the slope towards the big house. "Lexi – look!" she muttered between gritted teeth.

Lily had spotted Harry Finch standing by a back door watching them.

"Harry did it," Lexi decided in a flash. "He opened the gate and let the peacocks out – *on purpose!*"

Lily sighed. "What is his problem? I mean – why does he want to get us into trouble just because we came to feed Breezy? It doesn't make any sense."

Chapter Eight

"It sounds as if you're beginning to bond with Breezy," Miss Goodwin said.

It was Tuesday morning and she'd met Lily, Alfie and Lexi as she'd cycled home from the village shop.

The excited girls had hardly given themselves time to say hi before they'd shared the latest news about Rosemary Finch's foal.

"She was really shy at first but now we can go in and out of her stable without scaring her," Lily had explained.

71

"She even lets us stroke her!" Lexi had exclaimed.

"Bonding with an orphan foal is very tricky," Miss Goodwin reminded them with a smile. "I know because I did the same thing with Honeysuckle a long time ago."

"Did Honeysuckle's mother die too?" Lily asked as Miss Goodwin got off her bike and wheeled it up the path to Lighthouse Cottages.

"She did. I had to stay up all through the night, feeding Honeysuckle from a bottle every three hours."

Lexi's brown eyes lit up as she had an idea. "Would you like to come to the Hall with us and meet Summer Breeze?" she asked.

Lily nodded and smiled. "I'm sure Mr Finch won't mind."

So Miss Goodwin left her bike propped against her garden gate and walked on with them to Dentwood Hall.

"This is a very grand house." She was nervous as she walked with the girls across the lawn.

Lily led the way. "These are the stables. This is Monty. He was a racehorse."

Monty appeared at the door and stretched his handsome head towards the visitors.

"Hello, Monty," Miss Goodwin said as she patted his neck. "You're beautiful."

"And this is Phoebe." Lexi took her to the stable door to show her the cheeky Shetland pony.

"Very sweet," Miss Goodwin murmured.

"And Breezy!" Lily proudly announced.

For a few moments the old lady stood by the foal's door in silence. "She looks just like my Honeysuckle!" she said with a sigh. "She has the same lovely chestnut colouring and the white star . . ."

"Watch – she's not shy any more," Lexi said, easing her way into the stable.

Breezy came right up and nuzzled at Lexi's hand then she went to Lily, looking for her feed.

"Good!" Miss Goodwin studied Breezy closely. "You have to build her confidence bit by bit. Stroke and hug her as much as possible."

"Like this?" Lily asked, easing her arms around the foal's neck.

"Yes. Lexi, be careful not to stand behind her. Stay where she can see you. Now, Lily, run your hand along her back, pat her gently under her belly – yes, that's very good." Taking them step by step, Miss Goodwin guided Lily and Lexi in the art of winning the foal's trust.

* * *

By Tuesday lunch-time Lexi and Lily were cheerfully going in and out of Breezy's stable to stroke and pet her. At teatime the foal ate from the dish then skipped around her stable, rustling through the straw and kicking out her back legs for pure joy.

"You know what?" Lexi said. "She needs more space to play so why don't we bring her out of her stable?"

"Good idea," Lily said. She shot off to the tack room in search of the smallest head collar she could find and the handiest lead rope. "Will these do?"

"Let's see." Lexi took the head collar and showed it to Breezy. "I know – it smells funny," she murmured. "It's meant to go around your head like this. And this ring is where we clip on the lead rope – see!"

Slowly and surely Lexi buckled on the head collar while Lily held her breath.

The foal twitched and laid back her ears. Then she pricked them up again and looked cautiously at Lexi, as if to say *OK, what's next?*

"Follow me." Lexi clipped on the lead rope then gave a small pull.

Whoa! Breezy felt the tug of the rope and pulled back.

"Wait – I'll fetch some pellets," Lily told Lexi. She ran to the tack room and brought the grain back. She held the feed in her outstretched palm. "Here, Breezy – nice food!"

The foal flared her nostrils and took a step towards the door. Lexi pulled gently on the rope.

"Lovely, yummy pellets!" Lily urged, stepping backwards into the yard.

Greedy Breezy followed without even noticing the head collar or the rope.

Lily backed a few more steps until Lexi had led the foal out of the stable. "Good girl!" she breathed. She beamed at Lily.

Lily smiled as the foal took the feed from her hand.

"Huh!" Harry Finch scoffed. He'd appeared out of nowhere – jumped out on them while they worked.

Startled, Breezy shot back into her stable, almost pulling Lexi off her feet.

"What do you think you're doing?" Lily asked angrily.

"I'm watching you trying to make a pet of my mum's horse," he sneered while Lexi locked Breezy safely inside her stable. "If I

77

were you, I wouldn't bother."

"What do you mean?" First the sneaky trick with the peacocks and now this – Lexi was fed up with Harry and she didn't care if he knew it.

"She's not a pet," he told them. "And she never will be."

"Meaning what?" Lily felt her heart beat faster.

"Meaning her mother was a racehorse and so was her father," Harry told them. "And that's what Summer Breeze is going to be, so don't get too friendly. Before you know it she'll get sent to a trainer's yard and you'll never see her again!"

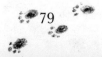

Chapter
Nine

Lily and Lexi trailed back to Sea View with Alfie. They hung their heads and didn't speak.

"Why so glum?" Matt asked as they walked into the kitchen. He'd finished work at his computer and was busy making dinner.

"Don't ask," Lexi sighed.

She and Lily slumped into chairs while Alfie hid quietly under the table.

"This is not like you," Matt said as he peeled an onion then chopped it. "Why aren't you whizzing to the computer and updating the website?"

"We're upset," Lily explained with a catch in her voice.

Her dad put down his knife and wiped his hands. "No one's ill, are they?" he asked. "Dino or Smudge, maybe?"

"No," Lexi sighed. "They're both fine."

"Breezy?"

"She's fine too." Taking a deep breath, Lily started to explain. "But Harry Finch just gave us some bad news."

"Mrs Finch isn't going to keep Breezy," Lexi broke in. "She'll get sent away."

Matt sat down at the table with them. "But not yet, surely? Isn't she far too young to go anywhere?"

"Harry wouldn't tell us," Lily told him, her grey eyes filling with tears. "All we know is, she's not going to stay at Dentwood Hall and be a normal horse that you can ride on the beach . . ."

"Or along the bridle paths . . ."

"Up on to the moors . . ."

"Or in the forest . . ."

"Stop!" Matt pleaded. "Does this mean that Rosemary is planning to sell her – which surely wouldn't be so bad if Breezy went to a nice, new owner."

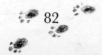

Lily and Lexi shook their heads. "No, it's worse than that!" they groaned. "Much worse!"

* * *

"Breezy has to be a racehorse. She'll be miserable," Lexi told her dad.

They hadn't stayed for dinner at Sea View because James said that Lexi looked tired and needed an early night. They'd gone home and by eight o'clock she had her pyjamas on, ready for bed.

Her dad came into her room. "Tell me again – what's going to happen to her."

"Mrs Finch is going to send her to a trainer's yard, whatever that is. It doesn't sound nice though."

"It's where they train thoroughbreds," he explained. "Listen – don't worry too much. They're usually smart places and the horses are properly looked after. They get fed well and every morning they're taken out onto the gallops."

"But it's like sending Alfie away," Lexi argued. "I'd never do that because I love him too much."

"But Alfie's a pet and Summer Breeze isn't," James pointed out.

Lexi frowned. "That's what Harry Finch said. He told us she's not a pet and she never will be."

"I guess he's right," her dad said softly. "It's Mrs Finch who owns that foal. She's the only one who can decide what happens to her – remember that."

* * *

Lily and Lexi both went to bed early but neither of them could sleep. They got up next day with heavy hearts.

As Lily got ready to go out and meet Lexi,

Jo stopped her and gave her some advice. "Dad says you're upset about Summer Breeze," she began.

"It's not fair, Mum!" Lily said. "Breezy's tiny and she needs lots of love!"

"I know, honey." Jo squeezed her hand. "But you must understand – these thoroughbreds are valuable. They're bred to win races, pure and simple."

Lily pictured poor little Breezy being loaded into a dark trailer. She thought of the bumpy journey and the strangers at the other end who would lead her out into a smart yard full of helpers and jockeys, all bustling about and being much too busy to make her feel at home. "It's just not fair," she moaned.

* * *

That morning Lily and Lexi didn't run with Alfie along the coastal path past Lighthouse

Cottages. Instead they dragged their feet towards Dentwood Hall and hardly noticed Miss Goodwin waving from her doorway.

"Girls, whatever is the matter?" she called as she came down the path and started to walk with them. She listened gravely as they explained. "But perhaps Harry's got it wrong or else he made it up just to upset you," she suggested. "I've seen him cycling along the path into the village and I've noticed he's not a very friendly boy."

Lily agreed. "But even Harry wouldn't make it up about the trainer's yard."

"Possibly not." Miss Goodwin thought hard. "Anyway I'm on your side – to my mind it does seem a rather harsh thing to do."

* * *

Lexi and Lily trudged on. They watched Alfie run ahead and saw Harry open the

Hall gate to let Molly out onto the path. As soon as he saw them he turned and went back into the garden.

"Woof!" Big Molly was happy to see her little friend. She barked and lolloped towards him, whirled around and wagged her tail.

Soon Alfie joined in the fun and together they raced out of sight.

"Harry Finch – just the person we *don't* want to see," Lexi groaned, slowing down even more.

Lily was the first to pull herself together. "Come on, forget about him. Let's go and feed Breezy," she decided.

She was first through the gate and surprised to find Harry hanging around to throw a ball for Molly and Alfie when normally he would have done his disappearing act. He threw and Alfie fetched.

He threw again. "Mum's here," he told Lexi and Lily as they crossed the lawn. "She came home early."

Sure enough, they found Rosemary Finch hard at work, hosing down the rubber matting in one of the empty stables. When she saw them arrive, she turned off the tap.

"Well done, girls!" she began without waiting for Lexi and Lily to say hello. "Harry tells me that you managed to get a head collar on Breezy while I was away. He says you made it look easy."

"He did?" Lily felt her cheeks go red.

He did? Lexi frowned and looked down at the water trickling from the hose. How come Harry Finch had said something nice about them?

"That's excellent news," Rosemary told them.

"So would you still like us to feed Breezy?" Lily asked. Perhaps Mrs Finch didn't need Muddy Paws any more.

"Yes, yes, of course. I have a hundred and one things to get on with while you do that." Rosemary set off towards Monty's stable then hesitated by Phoebe's door. "Is everything all right?" she asked.

"Yes, thank you." Lily reminded herself that she was here to do a job so she set off towards the tack room.

"Lexi?" Rosemary prompted.

Lexi wasn't as good as her cousin at pretending to be OK. As usual she came out with what was on her mind. "Mrs Finch, are you really going to send Breezy away?"

"Ah, I see – Harry must have told you!" As Phoebe poked her shaggy head over the door for a scratch and a stroke, Rosemary realized what was bothering the girls. "Yes, it's true."

"When?" Lexi felt her heart sink.

"I'm not sure yet, but that's what I've been doing these last two days," Rosemary explained. "I visited trainers' yards, looking for someone who would take Summer Breeze as a yearling."

"Did you find one?" Lexi swallowed hard. *Please say no! Say that you'll keep Breezy here!*

"I did. I found a top trainer on an excellent yard in Yorkshire. He says he'll take Breezy when she's twelve months old – perhaps before."

Yorkshire! That was hundreds and hundreds of miles away. And less than a year from now. Shaking her head in despair, Lexi followed Lily into the tack room.

Chapter Ten

As soon as the girls had fed Breezy they collected Alfie and got ready to head back to Sea View.

"How was she?" Harry lay in wait at the gate out on to the path.

"How was who?" Lexi asked glumly.

"Breezy."

What do you care? Lexi thought.

Lily pursed her lips. "She was fine, thanks," she replied. She didn't tell Harry how hard it had been to be in Breezy's stable, fluffing up the straw to make her bed comfy, petting and fussing her, not knowing how much longer she would enjoy this nice, easy life.

"I couldn't get near her," he admitted. "I did try though."

Lexi stared at him. "I didn't know that." In fact Rosemary had told her and Lily that Harry couldn't care less about horses.

"It's true," he insisted. "But I just made her jump and scared her so I gave up."

Hmm. Lily too was beginning to get a different impression of sulky, noisy, clumsy Harry. "Well, she's doing great now," she said, setting off after Lexi and Alfie along the cliff path.

* * *

On Wednesday afternoon Lily sat at the kitchen table and started a new list:

> Feed Smudge
>
> Call Jon and Sam

"I'll feed Smudge," Lexi offered straight away. "He likes boiled eggs, doesn't he?"

"Yeah, hamsters think they're yummy."

So Lexi boiled a pan of water and found the eggs while Lily made the call.

"Hi, Jon, this is Lily here from Muddy Paws."

"Hi, Lily. It's Sam, not Jon."

"Oops, sorry. Anyway, I was only ringing to ask about Harriet. Is there any news yet?"

"Not so far. She's still very fat and she's sleeping a lot. The vet says the babies could arrive any day now."

"OK, cool." Lily looked up to see her dad come into the kitchen holding a sheet of paper. "Thanks, Sam. I'll call again soon. Bye!"

"I thought you'd be interested in this," Matt said as he showed the girls a printout from a website. "It's information about a certain racehorse."

"Hey, this is Monty's picture!" Lexi cried as she recognized Rosemary Finch's handsome stallion. "Whoo, it says here he's worth sixty-five thousand pounds!"

"Sixty-five thousand!" Lily echoed as she read on. "And his father was a stallion called Red Kite and his mother was Montgomery Lass. Monty's real name is Montgomery Lad."

"He won four races on the flat before he retired," Matt added. "Total prize money was eighty-seven thousand pounds."

"Eighty-seven thousand!" Lily and Lexi echoed.

"It's an awful lot of money," Matt said. "And it certainly helps you to understand why Rosemary is keen to turn Breezy into another top class racehorse."

Lexi shook her head while Lily put into words what they were both thinking. "It's not about winning races," she said. "We just want Breezy to be happy!"

* * *

Make appointment for Jigsaw.

Lily was adding another job to the Muddy Paws list late on Wednesday afternoon when she looked out of the window in time to see Harry Finch walking towards the cottage.

Lexi saw him too. "What does he want?" she grumbled.

"I don't know but he's carrying something wrapped up inside a towel." Lily answered the door before Harry had time to knock.

He stopped short and gave a sharp gasp.

"What's wrong?" Lexi wanted to know.

"Ouch – he pricked me!"

"Who pricked you?" As Harry held up his bleeding finger, Lily stepped aside to let him come in. "What have you got inside the towel?"

"Quick, put it here." Lexi cleared a space on the table.

95

Slowly and carefully Harry placed his small bundle down.

Something was moving inside the towel and that something was prickly so it didn't take the girls long to work out what Harry had brought to Muddy Paws.

"Is it a hedgehog?" Lexi asked.

"A baby," he replied as he unwrapped the towel. "I found him on the path outside our gate after you left. He was all alone."

"Aah!" Lily caught sight of the baby hedgehog – a tiny, prickly dome with a sharp snout and beady black eyes. "Was he lost?"

Harry wiped his bloody finger on his jeans and nodded. "I didn't know what to do so I put food down to see if his mum would come. I waited ages."

"But she didn't show up?" Lexi prompted.

"No. Then Molly sniffed around a bit

under the hedge. She found a dead hedgehog
hidden in the grass. I looked but I couldn't
see how she died – there was no bleeding or
anything."

"You think it was his mum?" Lily
whispered.

The baby hedgehog blinked in the bright
light then quickly curled into a ball.

Harry nodded. "He's an orphan, just like
Breezy."

97

"Poor little thing." Lexi was already planning to find out what food they would give to a baby hedgehog.

"I thought you'd know what to do so I brought him here," Harry told them.

"Well, first we should keep him nice and warm." Lily went to a cupboard and brought back an empty shoe box. She lined it with newspaper and put a clean tea-towel on top to make a cosy bed.

"We need gloves!" Lexi ran outside to Matt's garden shed and came back with his thick leather gardening gloves. They were too big for her but she managed to lift the hedgehog and carefully put him in the box.

"That's better," Lily murmured. "Now we need to find some worms and beetles for him to eat."

"Worms and beetles? Are you sure?" Lexi

pulled a face and held back.

"Come on, Harry!" It was Lily's turn to run outside and raid the garden shed. She found two trowels and handed one to Harry. "Let's get digging!" she said.

* * *

"That's one happy little hedgehog." Lexi had punched airholes in the shoe box lid and was ready to put the roof on his cosy new house.

"He's been fed and now he's taking a snooze," Lily sighed. "Thanks, Harry. It looks like he'll be OK."

"So I'll leave him here with you?" he checked.

"You can if you like." Lexi was starting to think that maybe Harry wasn't so bad after all. "But definitely come back tomorrow and see how he's doing – OK?"

"Thanks." Harry blushed. He'd already

gone outside when he turned back. "There's something else."

Lily and Lexi waited on the doorstep.

"I want to say sorry," Harry mumbled from under the peak of his baseball cap.

"What for?" Lily asked.

"For the trick I played with the peacocks."

"That's OK," Lexi said slowly.

Harry cleared his throat. "And sorry for being mean about Breezy."

Whoa – it seemed Harry was keen to 'fess up big-time!

"I was mad when Mum gave you the job of looking after her," he said, almost too quietly for them to hear. "I wanted to do it."

"But your mum said you weren't interested in horses."

Harry shrugged and turned to walk away. "I had a go on Phoebe once or twice but

100

she bucked me off. It turned out I was a rubbish rider."

"Who says?" Lily asked.

"Dad was there both times. He told Mum I was useless – I heard him. They gave up on me after that."

Lily and Lexi thought of the clumsy, loud Harry they'd first met – always kicking a ball or clattering his bike down on the cobbles, yelling at the top of his voice. Now suddenly it had all changed and they felt sad for him.

"We're sorry – we didn't know any of that," Lexi said quietly.

He shrugged again. "Promise you won't tell anyone?"

"We promise," they said. "And we'll take care of your baby hedgehog – don't you worry!"

Chapter Eleven

"Still no news," Jon Simons told Lily when she rang early on Thursday.

"OK, but remember to tell us as soon as Harriet has the babies," she reminded him as he said goodbye.

The phone rang again as soon as she put it down. It was Lexi's turn to answer the call while Lily took a peek at Harry's baby hedgehog. "Hello, this is Muddy Paws. Lexi speaking."

"Lexi, good morning. Daisy Goodwin here."

"Hi!" Lexi could tell from Miss Goodwin's breezy tone that she had some good news to report. "How's Dino doing?"

"He's doing well, thank you. You wouldn't recognize him as the same timid creature you met earlier this week, thanks to your aromatherapy."

"That's cool," Lexi said.

"He rubs against my legs and purrs like the old Dino. When I left the door open for him earlier this morning, he even dared to set foot outside."

Lexi pictured the fluffy white Persian cat venturing out on to the path, one delicate step at a time. "That's really cool, Miss Goodwin."

"But that's *not* the reason I rang," the kind old lady went on. "I was sitting in the sun yesterday, remembering happy days with my lovely Honeysuckle, and I suddenly

remembered something I'd done with my own foal that you might like to try with Breezy."

Lexi listened carefully and took in every word.

"Lexi, my dear – you know when a farmer has a lamb whose mother has died he sometimes tries to pair it up with another ewe?"

"And he hopes that the new ewe will adopt the orphan?"

"Exactly. Well, I did something similar with Honeysuckle. At the time I had a friend who owned a mare called Dusty so I asked her if we could put Honeysuckle and Dusty together in the same paddock. We found that it was a nice arrangement for both of them – they made friends very quickly and Dusty became a kind of stepmother for Honeysuckle."

"So where would we find a stepmum for Breezy?"

"Right in front of your nose," Miss Goodwin reminded Lexi. "Think about it."

Suddenly Lexi got it. "You mean Pheebs!?" Phoebe, Rosemary Finch's cheeky Shetland.

"Pheebs?" Lily asked as she placed a dish of delicious beetles in the baby hedgehog's box and put the lid back on.

"Sshh!" Lexi hissed. "I'll explain later."

"Precisely," Miss Goodwin concluded. "Why not put Breezy and Phoebe out in a paddock together? I'm sure they'll have a wonderful time."

* * *

"The best place would be the small paddock behind the tack room," Rosemary suggested when Lily and Lexi explained their latest plan. "We don't use it much but there's

105

plenty of grass for Phoebe and Breezy to eat and we can easily keep an eye on them."

"So you think they'll get on OK?" Lily checked.

"We should try it at least." Busy with Monty as usual, Rosemary was willing for the girls to go ahead while she got ready for her ride. "Why not lead them both out there and see what happens?"

"Let's hope this works," Lexi said as she and Lily went to fetch head collars. "I'll take Pheebs out first and you can follow with Breezy."

"And I'll keep Molly and Alfie well out of the way," Harry offered. He took a ball out of his pocket and went on to the front lawn to play with the dogs.

"Was that my son, being nice for a change?" Rosemary commented as she put on Monty's saddle and fastened the girth. "Wonders will never cease."

Meanwhile, Lexi opened the door to the Shetland's stable. "OK, Pheebs," she began, "today we want you to be really good!"

Phoebe snickered and rubbed her nose against Lexi's arm.

"Yes, I know – you're totally cute. But are you listening to me? You have to be friendly with Breezy and not boss her about."

Phoebe made a burring noise with her lips then tossed her head.

"Remember, you're the grown up!" Lexi grinned as she fastened Phoebe's head collar and led her into the yard. "Ready?" she asked Lily who was waiting in Breezy's stable.

Lily nodded. "Go ahead, we'll follow you."

But Lily wasn't as calm as she sounded. After all, this was a challenge for Breezy –

being outside in the paddock with another horse. What if Phoebe didn't fancy the role of stepmum? She might be mean to Breezy and try to nip her, or even bite and kick? "Come on," she murmured and gave a gentle tug on the lead rope. "This is a *big* adventure!"

Slowly Breezy came out of her stable and took a good look around. She pricked her ears, watching carefully as Lexi led Phoebe out to the paddock.

"Let's go," Lily said, eager for the foal to take her first faltering steps.

Breezy trembled and pulled back towards her nice, safe stable.

"OK – no rush." Lily decided to wait.

Lexi was already at the gate with Phoebe. The paddock looked inviting with its white fencing and lush green grass so she opened the gate and led the lively Shetland pony in.

"Juicy grass, Pheebs!"

Yum! Phoebe tore at the grass with her teeth then munched happily.

Hmm – Lexi wondered what would happen if she took a handful of grass to Breezy.

Back in the yard, Lily took her time. "Don't worry – I know it looks scary out there but Pheebs will look after you," she promised Breezy and just at that moment the little Shetland raised her head and gave a welcoming neigh. "See!" Lily grinned.

So Breezy grew braver. She took a few steps across the yard.

"Good girl," Lily murmured. She smiled again as Breezy put in a playful hop and a skip. They'd crossed the yard and were walking down the side of the tack room when Lexi came towards them with a handful of grass.

"Nice grass – yummy-yum!" Lexi opened

her palm and held out the grass.

Breezy's nose twitched. She nibbled the blades – slowly at first then in one quick snatch and a big gulp. "There's lots more where that came from," Lexi promised, showing the foal the way.

Phoebe neighed again. *Come on in – there's plenty for both of us!*

Still Breezy hesitated. The wind ruffled

her tufty mane, the sun shone in her eyes. Oh but the grass smelled good! She picked up her hooves and trotted forward, past Lexi straight into the paddock.

"Excellent, girls – well done!" Rosemary had watched it all from a distance. She heard the click as Lexi shut the gate and Lily took off Breezy's head collar. She saw Phoebe come up and give Breezy a friendly nudge with her nose, smiled as the little foal grew bold and with another hop, skip and jump broke into a jerky canter around the paddock.

Wheee – freedom!

* * *

Lexi and Lily decided it was safe to leave Breezy in the paddock with Phoebe all morning.

"Miss Goodwin's plan worked," Lily told Harry as they took a walk along the cliff path with Molly and Alfie. "Phoebe didn't try to boss Breezy around and Breezy is much less scared when Pheebs is there!"

"They're happy together," Lexi sighed.

They reached the wooden steps to the beach and looked down on the stretch of smooth sand with the waves crashing on to the shore.

Alfie yapped and ran down the first few

steps but Lexi shook her head. "Sorry, it's nearly lunch-time," she told him. "We have to get back."

So they turned for home and talked about Harry's baby hedgehog.

"Wouldn't you like to look after him yourself?" Lily suggested as the two dogs ran ahead.

"What would I feed him besides worms and beetles?"

"You could give him bread soaked in warm milk."

"OK – maybe," he said, slowly getting used to the idea.

"And have you thought of a name?" Lexi wondered. "Spike, maybe? Spikes – prickles – hedgehogs – get it?"

Harry shook his head. "I like Solo."

"Because he was lost and all alone when

you found him. Yeah, Solo!" Lily agreed.

And they hurried back to Dentwood Hall to bring Phoebe and Breezy in from the paddock.

* * *

The side gate was closed and from the garden the three peacocks let out their shrill call.

Harry opened the gate.

"E-e-elp!"

"That's weird – it sounds like they're saying 'Help'." For some unknown reason Lexi gave a small shudder. She watched Alfie and Molly run up the sloping lawn towards the house. Then her eyes were drawn to the paddock.

"It's empty!" Lily gasped.

"It can't be!" Lexi could hardly believe her eyes. "Where are Breezy and Pheebs?"

Harry, Lexi and Lily began to run across

114

the lawn. It was true – the horses had vanished from the paddock.

"Maybe your dad took them back to their stables," Lily suggested.

Harry shook his head. "Dad's gone to work. And look at that!" He pointed to a break in the white wooden fence.

Lexi groaned and kept on running. The fence was rotten. There was a gap that was easily big enough for two small horses to get through.

Lily reached the fence first. She saw hoofprints in the soft soil and strands of long white hair caught in the nearby hedge – hair from Phoebe's mane or tail.

"They must have pushed against the fence and broken it," Harry sighed.

But how long ago? And where were they now? Lexi's and Lily's hearts thumped against their ribs. They were so scared that they could hardly breathe.

Stepping through the gap in the broken fence, Lexi looked down from the footpath on to sheer cliffs and an empty beach. There wasn't even a hedge – just a wonky barbed-wire fence to keep Phoebe and Breezy from falling on to the rocks below.

"Quick, we have to find them!" Lily cried.

Without a word Harry turned and raced towards the house.

"Where's he going?" Lexi frowned.

But there was no time to worry about Harry. With their hearts in their mouths, Lilly and Lexi set off along the narrow path towards Lighthouse Cottages.

Chapter Twelve

"Miss Goodwin, have you seen Breezy and Phoebe?" Lily cried when she saw the old lady sitting in the sun with Dino on her lap. "They escaped from the paddock!"

Dino had to jump to the ground as Daisy Goodwin stood up. "Oh dear," she sighed. "That's bad news. But no, I'm sorry – they didn't come this way."

"Maybe they went in the other direction," Lexi suggested, turning and running back the way they'd come.

To their surprise the girls bumped into

Harry as they arrived back at the Hall.

"I brought these," he gasped, holding up two head collars.

So that was where he'd gone. "Good thinking," Lily told him.

As Harry stopped to draw breath he spotted his mum riding Monty into the stable yard. "Should we tell her?" he asked.

"No, there's no time." Lexi asked Harry to show Breezy's head collar to Alfie. "Find Breezy," she told her clever little dog.

Alfie sniffed at the head collar, put his nose to the ground and sniffed again. Head down and tail up, he followed a scent and soon Molly joined in.

"Let's go!" Lily told Harry. "And try not to look down – it's too scary."

They chased after the dogs along the narrow path, round bends and over a small wooden bridge where a stream tumbled over the cliff-face down on the rocks far below.

"Don't look down!" Lily repeated. Her heart thumped. *Please let Breezy and Pheebs be OK!* she prayed.

Alfie and Molly charged on out of sight. Molly gave a deep woof, Alfie let out a high yip and up ahead a horse gave a shrill neigh. Harry, Lily and Lexi chased the dogs round the bend . . .

"Phoebe!" Lexi cried.

"Thank goodness!" Lily breathed a sigh of relief while Harry went up to the Shetland and put on her head collar.

"But where's Breezy?" Lexi asked. The path ahead grew rocky. There was no sign of the foal.

Phoebe tossed her head. Alfie and

Molly sniffed the ground and picked up another scent.

"I'll take Phoebe home," Harry told the girls as he led Phoebe back towards the Hall.

So Lily, Lexi and the two dogs went on with the search. A strong breeze blew up from the sea and clouds blocked out the sun. Alfie and Molly slowed down. They stopped, sniffed here and there, turned around and went back the way they'd come until they reached the bridge with the tumbling stream.

"Why have we come back?" Lily had run so fast that she thought her lungs would burst. Her throat felt dry, her heart pounded.

"Alfie and Molly have found something." Lexi left the path and tried to follow. She had to trample through long grass and push bushes aside.

"What can you see?" Lily called. The

undergrowth grew so thick that she couldn't make anything out. She heard Lexi tell Alfie to stay down then she saw Molly break out of the bushes to show her a way back in.

Lily followed Molly. The thorn bushes pricked her hands and face. She went down on to her hands and knees and crawled forward.

"Sshh!" Lexi hissed as she heard Lily crawl through the bushes.

When Lily made it to where Lexi crouched beside Alfie she gave a little cry.

There was Breezy, teetering at the edge of a rock on the far bank of the stream. Her ears were flat against her head, her eyes rolling with fright.

Lily looked down at the gushing water. It was too steep and too deep to cross. "What do we do now?" she asked Lexi.

"We can't make any sudden moves," Lexi pointed out. "I say we crawl back through the bushes and use the bridge – see if we can get to her from the far side of the stream."

It was the only choice they had and Lily saw that Lexi was right. But it was risky. The place where Breezy stood was so wet and slippery that she could easily fall. "We're coming to get you," she called to the terrified foal as she and Lexi decided to backtrack once more.

Breezy shifted her weight. She almost slipped from her rocky ledge.

Lily's and Lexi's stomachs lurched.

Then quickly they fought their way back through the thorn bushes, slipping and sliding through mud until they reached the path and ran across the narrow bridge with Alfie and Molly.

Then they heard voices along the path, saw Harry sprinting towards them carrying a head collar, with Rosemary Finch following close behind.

"Be careful, Harry!" Rosemary warned as he leaped from the path on to a rock and scrambled up the slope.

He climbed from rock to rock, until he perched above the rushing stream.

"It's dangerous!" his mum called. "Harry, please take care!"

"It's OK – I can get to Breezy from here," he called to Lily and Lexi as he stepped across a gap between rocks then disappeared into the bushes.

The girls met Mrs Finch on the path. They held their breaths and waited for what seemed like forever. Then they saw the bushes move and heard twigs snap. They

caught sight of Harry's white baseball hat, a glimpse of a chestnut brown coat. Still they held their breaths.

"Come on, Breezy – you can do it!" Harry murmured. He pushed branches aside. "That's right – good girl!"

And they appeared at last – first Harry then Breezy. They staggered out of the bushes, across the rocks towards Lily, Lexi and Rosemary.

"It's OK – she's fine," Harry told them.

"Brilliant!" Lexi wanted to run and hug him but instead she picked Alfie up and kissed him on the head.

"Fantastic!" Lily beamed.

"Harry, you amaze me," Rosemary Finch said as she stood back and watched her son lead Breezy home. "You truly do!"

Chapter Thirteen

"Mum, you should've seen what Harry did this morning!" The girls were back at Sea View, tripping over each other to bring Jo and Matt up to date.

"He was a superhero!" Lexi exclaimed. "He climbed up some rocks and rescued Breezy. Honestly, you should've seen him!"

Jo was puzzled. "This is Harry Finch we're talking about – right?"

"Harry Finch – the boy who plays mean tricks and doesn't like Breezy?" Matt winked at Jo and waited for an answer.

"Harry's cool," Lily insisted. "His mum and dad thought he didn't care about Breezy but it turns out he really he does."

"We were scared she was going to fall but Harry climbed up to rescue her," Lexi explained.

Lily pointed to Solo's box. "Plus, he found this baby hedgehog and now he's building a nest box for him."

"We're taking Solo back to Dentwood Hall straight after lunch," Lexi told them.

"Very good," Jo nodded. She looked at her watch. "Uh-oh, it's time for me to get back to the café."

"And I've got work to do too." Matt opened his laptop. "Oh, I nearly forgot – the Simons twins rang while you were out. They said to tell you that Harriet has had her babies."

* * *

When the girls arrived at the Hall with Alfie they heard the sound of hammering from inside the tack room.

"Hi, Monty, hi, Pheebs!" Lexi called into the stables as she ran by.

Lily followed more slowly, carrying Solo inside his cosy cardboard box. "Hi, Breezy!" she murmured, stopping to check in on the rescued foal.

Breezy came to the door and poked her nose over the top. Lily smiled and stroked her then walked on.

"Harry – hi!" Lexi called.

He came to the tack room door with a hammer in his hand. "Mum and I are making Solo's nest box. We've nearly finished. Do you want to see?"

Lexi and Lily left Alfie outside and went

128

in. "Hi, Mrs Finch."

Proudly Harry showed off a wooden box with a length of plastic piping fitted to a hole in the side. "This is a tunnel for Solo to use as a way in and out," he explained. "Now we just have to line it with sawdust and leaves then nail the lid on and it's ready."

"A five-star hedgehog hotel." Rosemary smiled as she left the tack room. "We'll finish this later, Harry. Right now I have to go and check on the workmen."

"They're mending the paddock fence," Harry explained.

"So where will you put Solo's new home?" Lily asked as she placed the box on a table in the corner of the tack room.

"I don't know. Come and help me decide." He led the way outside but as he walked past Breezy's stable the smile slipped from his face and he grew serious.

Lily thought she understood why. "I know," she sighed. "You're like us – you wish that she could stay here forever."

He nodded.

"But your mum won't let her?" Lexi asked. "Breezy still has to go to Yorkshire and live with strangers?"

Again he nodded and a frown formed between his eyes.

"Hey, Breezy!" Lily peered over the door into the foal's stable. "We all want you to stay here, you know that – don't you?"

Eagerly the foal came up and gave the door a small let-me-out kick.

"Just like Monty," Lexi sighed. "You're a fast learner. How about we take you for a walk?"

So they fastened Breezy's head collar and

Harry walked her towards the paddock where the workmen were packing up their tools.

Breezy's hooves had hardly touched the grass before she jumped and skipped for joy.

"We want you to stay here and grow up with Monty and Pheebs," Lily confided as Rosemary walked towards them. "We don't want you to be a racehorse. We want you to live with Harry."

"And go on the bridle paths and play on the beach." It was a dream that Lexi didn't think could come true. Still, she crossed her fingers and prayed.

"The fence is mended," Rosemary told them. "You can let Breezy off the lead rope if you like."

So Harry unclipped the rope and they stood back to watch.

Breezy stepped forward to snatch a mouthful of grass. Then she hopped and skipped, ran then munched again.

"She seems happy enough." Rosemary stooped to pat Alfie then folded her arms and looked thoughtful.

Harry hung his head. He kicked the ground with the toe of his trainer.

"You did well this morning," she told her son. "You were very brave."

Lily sneaked a look at Lexi. Could they dare to hope?

Breezy trotted and jumped until she came full circle, back to where they stood. She trotted up to Harry and nudged his arm.

"Of course, I would have to have a serious talk with your dad before I made any decision." Rosemary seemed to be thinking aloud.

Breezy nuzzled Harry's chest. *Stroke me!*

He gave a sad little smile and patted her neck.

"I would tell him that I've had a serious change of heart about Breezy's future."

Lily and Lexi held their breaths.

"But I would explain how brave you were," Rosemary went on. "And how wrong *we* were."

Yes! The girls' eyes shone. What they

133

wished for was actually coming true!

Harry looped his arm around Breezy's neck and smiled again as she nuzzled the cap from his head. The cap fell on to the grass and Rosemary stooped to pick it up. "I think your dad will listen to me," she told him quietly.

He let out a big sigh then for the first time looked his mum in the eye. "Does this mean Breezy won't have to go to the trainer's yard?" he murmured, hoping against hope.

"And she won't have to be a racehorse?" Lexi jumped in.

"She can stay here after all?" Lily asked.

There was a long, long pause as Rosemary made up her mind. "Yes, she can," she agreed. "Breezy can be your horse, Harry. It's clear as day that you love her and she loves you."

"Harriet!" Lily suddenly remembered.

They'd walked Breezy back to her stable then said goodbye to Harry and Rosemary. Now she, Lexi and Alfie were on the footpath, greeting Miss Goodwin as they passed Lighthouse Cottages.

"Is everything all right up at the Hall?" she asked from her doorway.

"Everything's brilliant, thanks!" Lexi waved and ran on. "Breezy can stay with Harry – yippee!"

But now Muddy Paws had other things to do and finding homes for the guinea pig's babies was at the top of Lily's never-ending list.

"Let's go and see them," Lexi suggested. "I haven't seen baby guinea pigs before."

"Me neither," Lily said. "I bet they're tiny."

"Teenie-weenie."

"All skinny and pink."

"And wrinkled." Lexi turned off the cliff path towards the village green where Jon and Sam Simons lived. "They'll be absolutely gorgeous," she cried. "Come on, Alfie, we can't wait!"

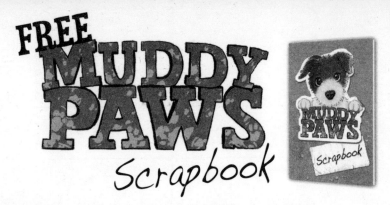

FREE MUDDY PAWS Scrapbook

Find out what happens to Lexi and Lily in *Coaching Madcap* – another Muddy Paws adventure – and receive a FREE Muddy Paws scrapbook! The scrapbook is the ideal place for you to put pictures of all your favourite animals and pets. Plus there are activities perfect for all Muddy Paws fans!

To receive your Muddy Paws scrapbook, you need to collect two tokens. One is below and you'll find another token in *Coaching Madcap*. Then simply fill in the form on this page and send it to us with both tokens and we'll send you your FREE Muddy Paws scrapbook!

Send one completed form and two tokens to: The Muddy Paws Scrapbook Offer, The Marketing Department, Hachette Children's Books, 338 Euston Road, London, NW1 3

Closing date: 31 January 2014

TERMS AND CONDITIONS

(1) Open to UK and Republic of Ireland residents only (2) You must provide the email address of a parent or guardian for your entry to be valid (3) Photocopied tokens are not accepted (4) The form must be completed fully for your entry to be valid (5) Scrapbooks ar distributed on a first come, first served basis while stocks last (6) No part of the offer is exchangeable for cash or any other offer (7) Please allow 28 days for delivery (8) Your details will only be used for the purposes of fulfilling this offer and, if you choose [see ti box below], to receive email newsletters about other great Hachette Children's books, and will never be shared with any third party.

- - - - - - - - ✂ - - - - - - - -

Please complete using capital letters (UK Residents Only)

ONE TOKE

FIRST NAME:

SURNAME:

DATE OF BIRTH: DD|MM|YYYY

ADDRESS LINE 1:

ADDRESS LINE 2:

ADDRESS LINE 3:

POSTCODE:

PARENT OR GUARDIAN'S EMAIL:

☐ I'm happy to receive email newsletters and information about other great Hachette Children's books (I can unsubscribe at any time).

www.hachettechildrens.